Fire Chief Fran

Linda Ashman   Illustrations by **Nancy Carpenter**

ASTRA YOUNG READERS

AN IMPRINT OF ASTRA BOOKS FOR YOUNG READERS

New York

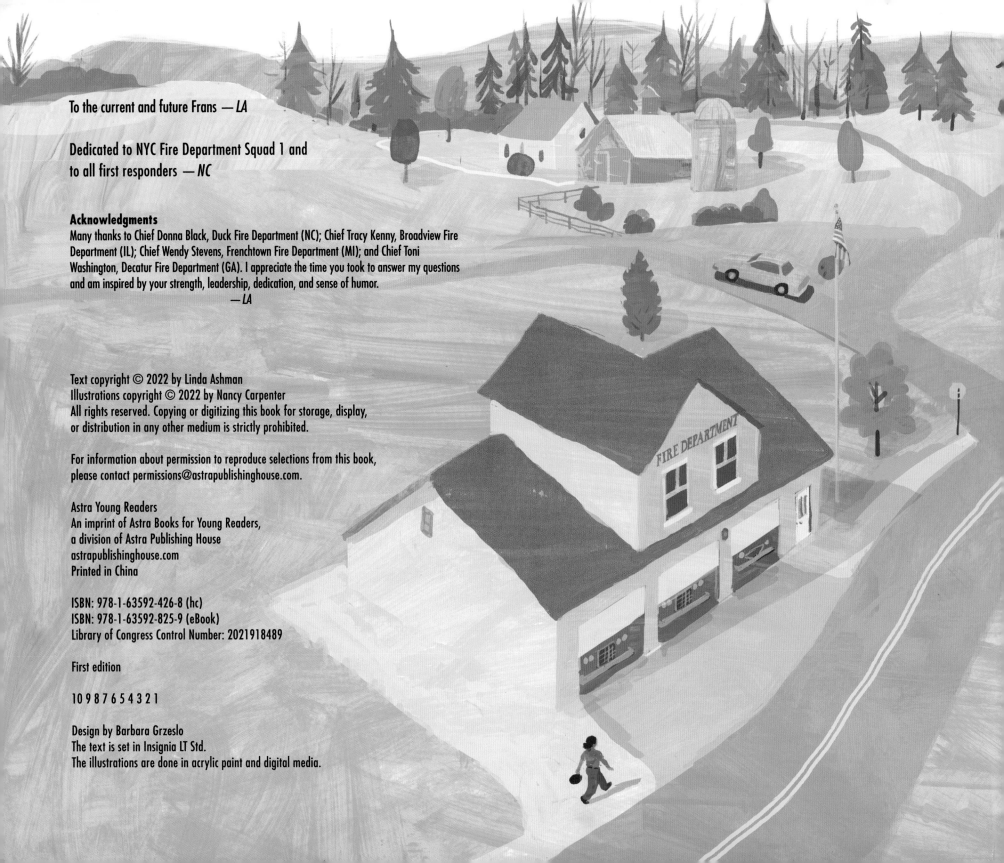

To the current and future Frans — *LA*

Dedicated to NYC Fire Department Squad 1 and
to all first responders — *NC*

Acknowledgments
Many thanks to Chief Donna Black, Duck Fire Department (NC); Chief Tracy Kenny, Broadview Fire
Department (IL); Chief Wendy Stevens, Frenchtown Fire Department (MI); and Chief Toni
Washington, Decatur Fire Department (GA). I appreciate the time you took to answer my questions
and am inspired by your strength, leadership, dedication, and sense of humor.
— *LA*

Astra Young Readers
An imprint of Astra Books for Young Readers,
a division of Astra Publishing House
astrapublishinghouse.com
Printed in China

ISBN: 978-1-63592-426-8 (hc)
ISBN: 978-1-63592-825-9 (eBook)
Library of Congress Control Number: 2021918489

First edition

10 9 8 7 6 5 4 3 2 1

Design by Barbara Grzeslo
The text is set in Insignia LT Std.
The illustrations are done in acrylic paint and digital media.

Fire Chief Fran meets with her crew.
It's a new shift—
there's so much to do!

The trucks are inspected above and below.
The tools and equipment are ready to go.

Then...
lights begin flashing,
and—**CLANG!**—the bells blast.
They leap into action—
they need to move **FAST!**

Ms. Robinson's puppy chased after a duck—
straight into a fence.
Now Bruno is stuck.

Ever so gently, the chief frees the pooch.
Bruno says thanks with a wag and a smooch.

Back at the station . . . the team works in pairs—
lunging and lifting and sprinting up stairs.

Says Fire Chief Fran, "We need to stay fit.
Fighting a fire takes power and grit!"

Then. . .

lights begin flashing,
and—**CLANG!**—the bells blast.
They leap into action—
they need to move **FAST!**

The Millers were camping in Cedar Falls Park.
The brush was ignited with one tiny spark.

The chief and her crew work through the haze,
aiming their hoses, dousing the blaze.

Back at the station . . . it's time for a tour.
Mr. Lee's class pours through the door.
They check out the pumpers, the nozzles, and tools,
while Fire Chief Fran shares safety rules:

"Don't play with matches. Or lighters. Or gas.
And don't start a fire near dry leaves and grass!"

Then . . .
lights begin flashing,
and—**CLANG!**—the bells blast.
They leap into action—
they need to move **FAST!**

Two players collided—*THUMPITY THUMP*.
Luke has a bruise. Cam has a bump.
They're iced up and bandaged and eager to play.
"Thank you!" they holler. The rig drives away.

Back at the station . . . they're practicing drills.
Training for rescues, improving their skills.
"A twister, a crash, a flood or a fall—
we have to be ready, whatever the call!"

Then...

lights begin flashing,
and—**CLANG!**—the bells blast.
They leap into action—
they need to move **FAST!**

It's rainy and windy.
A tree's fallen down.
It's blocking North Main.
The crew zooms to town.

They work through the storm, clearing the site.
"Thanks!" call the drivers. "Have a good night!"

Back at the station . . . they prep for a meal—
they simmer and stir, boil and peel.

At last, dinner's ready.
They each grab a plate,
begin to dish up—
but this meal has to wait,

when...
lights begin flashing,
and—**CLANG!**—the bells blast.
They leap into action—
they need to move **FAST!**

It's Charlie's Café—
there's smoke in the sky.
The cars pull aside as the rig races by.

The ladder goes up.
The chief scrambles higher—
helps Charlie escape
while they put out the fire.

"Thank you!" calls Charlie.
He waves to the crew.
"You're welcome," they answer.
"That's what we do."

Fire Chief Fran knows they all work their best
with food and some fun
and plenty of rest.

They read and relax,
then lights out at ten.